Chris Best is now retired, a keen gardener, energetic walker and enjoys travelling, however, during the winter he started to write. The inspiration for his first book came from a regular car journey with his youngest daughter, Ashleigh when they created together the '*Giganta Moles.*'

Ashleigh Best has always had an interest in being creative by painting and drawing. In 2017, she travelled to Australia for a year, but upon her arrival home, her father, Chris, surprised her with having written the story that they always spoke about writing. Since then, Ashleigh has worked in the legal profession, enjoys socialising in the sun, travelling, and cuddling any animal that is around.

To my children and grandchildren who enabled me to find
and indulge in my 'inner storyteller'.

Chris Best and Ashleigh Best

# GIGANTA MOLES – A NEW BEGINNING

AUSTIN MACAULEY PUBLISHERS™

LONDON • CAMBRIDGE • NEW YORK • SHARJAH

A CIP catalogue record for this title is available from the British Library.

ISBN 9781528973236 (Paperback)
ISBN 9781528973250 (ePub e-book)

www.austinmacauley.com

First Published 2022
Austin Macauley Publishers Ltd®
1 Canada Square
Canary Wharf
London
E14 5AA

To my wife, Madeline, for her patience while I spent hours typing at the computer without her knowing what I was doing. To her being the first to read my efforts and her valuable comments about my writing and first proof reading. To my daughter, Ashleigh, for her initial ideas many years ago and now more recently, helping with the story. – Chris Best.

To my dad, Chris, for always listening to me talking hours of nonsense on our drives. You have never stopped encouraging me to strive for more and without you, this story would have been lost in our memories. – Ashleigh Best

# Table of Contents

# 1. The Clawfoots' Arrival

The days were starting to lengthen and it felt like the coldest weather had gone for this Winter. All of a sudden, there appeared to be some sort of disturbance down by the river. The river wound its way down the wide bottomed valley, passing through woods and dividing fields. The disturbance was at the bottom of the field by the wood. The birds were all shouting their warning and the squirrels were scampering about the branches high above. They would stop every now and again to look down into the field. There was also movement just inside the wood. They look alarmed, but then, they were not sure what to do. Some start to move away into the wood before turning and coming back. It's as though they are afraid and yet, not. A couple of deer further up the field had stopped eating and stood watching. They were transfixed by something. Their ears held firmly upright, listening to all the noises in case they sensed danger. They needed to be alert so if necessary, they could make a quick exit into the woodland undergrowth.

All the other noises that could be heard, were as you would expect. There were cars travelling along the road a couple of fields away and a tractor moving about the farm yard at the top of the field. Some distant cows could be heard and the bleat of sheep on the other side of the river. All appears to be normal, apart from a small area down by the river.

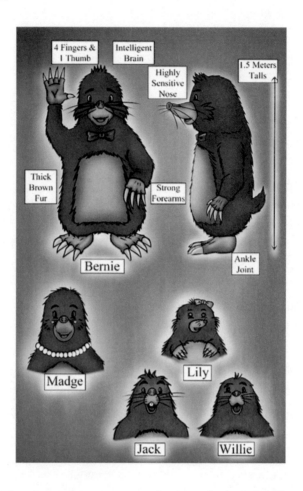

The commotion turns out to be the arrival of The Clawfoot Family. They are giganta moles. A species of mammal that very few people have ever seen before. Considering their size and their busyness, it is no wonder the animals and birds are somewhat alarmed. They feel they must be dangerous and yet, they do not look to attack or chase anything. They do not know what they are or what their intentions will be. For now, they must just keep their distance and a watchful eye on them, until they can determine whether they are friend or foe.

Giganta moles are large. A fully grown male, which is generally larger than the females, can reach 1.5 meters in length. They have the ability to walk upright, when they are not confined to their underground tunnels, but are very happy walking on all fours. They are able to do this due to their extraordinary ankle joint on their rear limbs, which can rotate to accommodate their duel walking styles. They are covered in a dark brown fur, which keeps them warm in the Winter and will moult slightly in the Spring, as the weather warms. Their Summer coat, although a little thinner, still retains its dark brown colour.

Their forearms are very strong and have hands rather than paws, each with five digits, like our fingers. These "fingers" are also very strong with claw-like nails which allow them to dig through the soil to make their homes. Their thumb joint is similar to humans, as they use this to grip.

Oh, they are also very intelligent and are able to communicate with most animals, as they have mastered the art of learning the language of the various animals that live around them.

The Clawfoots' had decided to move house and they were seriously thinking of making the area close to the woods and just above the river, their new home. It would appear that the ground was soft enough to dig easily. It was under the branches of the larger trees that edged the field, which meant the farmer would not plough this part of the field. It was near to the river for drinking water, plus they could swim there on a warm Summers day to cool down. Perfect. That was the conclusion of Bernie with approval from Madge, his wife.

Bernie, Dad, is about 1.5 metres tall with dark brown fur. He has very powerful arms and legs which are especially useful when building your own home. He is 10 years old, which may seem young to have a family, but their life expectancy is a lot shorter than humans, at around 40 years. The shape of his head is similar to humans, although the eyes are more sunken with bushy eyebrows above and a slightly longer nose, which is black. The mouth is in proportion to the face and the teeth are a mixture of incisors, canines and molars, which reflect their diet. Bernie is quite serious in outlook, often appearing to look unhappy. He takes looking after his young family very seriously and is extremely protective of them. As already mentioned, giganta moles are very intelligent and Bernie is exceptionally so. He is able to speak to most creatures, including humans, and is able to pick up a new language very quickly.

On a lighter note, Bernie loves playing and swimming during the Summer months. The cool water helps him cope with the warm weather as giganta moles will only moult slightly in the Summer. The other main reason he likes the water is that he loves playing with his children. He often likes to bomb drop near them from the bank or surprising them by swimming up to them under water. They play a game like water polo by using puff balls as the ball and marking each bank to show where the goals are. It can get a little rough sometimes so they have to have a stock of puff balls, as they often get smashed.

Madge, Mum, is a little shorter than Bernie at about 1.4 metres in height and her fur is slightly lighter. She also has very powerful arms and legs. She is 10 years old and has known Bernie all her life. They grew up together in the same woods some miles from where they are now. It was a small group of four families living deep inside a large wooded valley, where they hardly ever saw humans. It was a peaceful place where all the children had many miles of woodland to play in and many streams to jump over or swim in to cool down in the Summer. She is a very organised and tidy giganta mole, keeping the house in order and making sure the children put their things away. She is generally more relaxed than Bernie, but is always alert to any possible danger. She always feels that life is for living.

She really has proved to be a good mother to her three children, twin boys and a daughter, who is the youngest child. Madge has loved raising them but her slight problem now was that the twins were getting older and did not want or need her constant supervision. She knew she would have to start letting them go on a longer leash and before long, let go altogether. Madge is a very sociable creature and can often be found having a chat with a neighbour or someone just passing through the area they live in. It keeps her informed of what is going on in the area, was her reasoning, although Bernie knew it was just that she likes to talk. Playing in the water is another great pastime for her in the Summer for the same reasons as Bernie. In fact, it was from their childhood games that they both got such a love for the water. One final point of interest is that Madge can sing. It is one of the many things Bernie loves about Madge. She will sing most of every day and joins in with the birds, imitating their songs as well. It always proves to be a surprise to all the new animals they come across.

The children were eying up the woods and could sense a whole lot of fun exploring the woodland, along with meeting their new neighbours. They did however get the feeling that the locals were a little wary of them. Strange they thought, but were soon distracted as Dad called for them.

# 2. Digging Their Home

Bernie had called everyone together to explain that this was where they are now going to live and they need to start digging out their new home. He would start by digging a tunnel that would run along the side of the wood. He needed the twins to move the soil he throws out and spread it out along the edge of the wood. This was to keep their entrance clear. Madge would take Lily into the woods to find a suitable exit point for their home, in case of emergencies. They always have an emergency exit in case of danger, plus it gives an air flow through their home. Once Madge has located a suitable exit point, she would dig a small hole as a marker. Bernie would then mark where he wanted Madge to aim for with her digging, as this was where they would join the two tunnels. This exit point would be covered over with fallen branches and leaves to conceal the hole. They do not want anything to discover their escape route and fill it in or indeed, for another animal to think they have luckily discovered a new home, already built for them.

Bernie dug furiously, throwing large amounts of soil out for the twins to move away from the entrance. As he moved further under the ground, the twins had to start working in a line, as the soil from Bernie did not reach the entrance. Jack

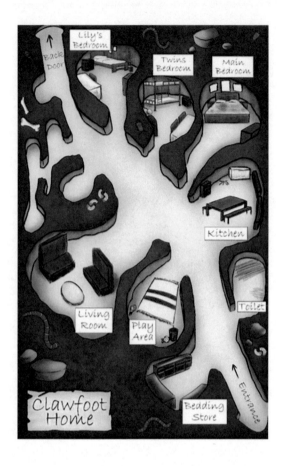

would be inside the tunnel and moved the soil to the entrance, while Willie moved it onto the growing pile alongside the wood. It was hard work, but they all knew that they must get the tunnel dug and also the escape route before dark. It would not be safe to sleep in the tunnel without an effective escape route and so without any complaining, the twins kept on working without a break. They knew their Dad would stop for a break eventually and they would have something to eat.

As Bernie dug, he kept a keen eye open for any worms or beetles. When he found one, he put it in his pouch that was attached to his belt. This would be their lunch and he hoped the twins were also keeping a sharp eye out for these tasty morsels. He knew Madge would be doing the same while she dug the small hole somewhere in the wood. He needed to go about 10 metres in from the entrance, so there would be enough room to make the side chambers, which would be their living quarters.

The side chambers or rooms would consist of three bedrooms, a living area where they would also eat, a food store and an area for a toilet. The positions of these and their size would be determined by Madge as she liked to design the layout of the home and the furnishings. These chambers would be dug out in the days to come.

Madge called to Bernie from the entrance of the tunnel to find out how he was getting on and also to say she had managed to collect quite a lot of worms and beetles. Bernie stopped digging and moved back towards the entrance pushing the last of the soil he had loosened. When he reached the tunnel entrance, the twins moved the soil onto the pile. Bernie blinked as the sun blinded him briefly. He had been digging for a good hour and his eyes were used to the dark. This sudden brightness made him stop until his eyes adjusted.

'That's better,' Bernie said after a few seconds. 'I can now see you all. Wow, what a pile you have made boys. I think we will need to spread it about a bit, otherwise we will draw the attention of the farmer. I don't want him down here at the moment, as I haven't finished and we will have nowhere to hide safely.'

'How far have you got?' asked Madge.

'About eight meters I think,' replied Bernie. 'Let's have some lunch and then you can have a look and see how much further you would like me to go.'

They sat at the edge of the wood, but still in the sun, so they could enjoy the warmth. There was a slight breeze, but as this was coming from the direction of the wood, they were sheltered from it. Not a bad day at all really. They all tucked in to their lunch without any further words. It was hungry work digging out a new home, plus they had walked a few hours before this, searching for a suitable place to live.

Moving home is not something giganta moles do lightly. Once they have found a suitable place, they like to make friends with all the neighbourhoods' animals, so they can feel safe. They believe that if they work with their neighbours, then they should all be safe, as they would look out for each other and warn of any dangers. To be honest, giganta moles have very few predators and those would not attack them without good reason. Giganta moles are very effective at protecting themselves.

The Clawfoots had to move, not due to predators, but because of man. They do not consider man as a predator, although they are very wary of them and treat them with the greatest respect. They had lived very comfortably all their lives some miles away but just recently man had moved large machinery into the field and had begun to dig up the soil. They could not work out what they were doing as they had never seen machinery like this before. They were used to farmers ploughing, fertilising and harvesting the crops with all manner of equipment. Even strange machinery to round up sheep and cattle that were not tractors but which moved very quickly. These however, were new to them. They had noticed the men looking at the entrance of their home and they felt it would be safer to move out before the machines came further across the field.

So they were here and so far, there had been no sign of the farmer. They had heard movement up by the farm buildings but no one had ventured across the field. The local animals were numerous, but so far had kept their distance. This would change once they had got their home sorted and the children went out exploring and playing. Like all children, they are not afraid to speak to other children. It takes no time at all to get to know neighbours, when you have children.

Bernie stood up and stretched. He could feel the stiffness in his joints from this morning's digging. He put it to the back of his mind as he still had a long way to go.

'Come on,' he said, 'we need to get going, otherwise it will be dark before we are finished.'

He went into the burrow with Madge to see how much further she wanted him to dig. She agreed that another couple of metres would do and then she left to join Lily at the entrance. The boys had followed their mum and dad so they would be ready to remove the dirt. Madge and Lily waited just outside the hole ready to remove the soil from the entrance and add it to the pile the boys had already made. It wasn't long before the boys came out of the hole pushing a large amount of soil before them with Bernie following on behind.

'That's about it, Madge,' he said. 'I need to see where you have started to dig our escape exit, so I know the direction I need to dig, to meet up with you.'

They walked into the wood with Bernie pacing out in the direction he had dug underground. Once he had reached the point where he believed he had dug to, Madge headed off with

Lily towards where she had started to dig. When Madge and Lily had reached the small hole Madge had dug, they turned to face Bernie. They were about 20 metres away with a clear run between the trees.

'That's a great position Madge,' shouted Bernie. 'There are no trees in the way, which will save us a lot of time. I will get Jack to put a large stick in the ground when we have determined the exact position of the tunnel here, so you have a point to aim for. I will now go back into the tunnel and start to dig towards you.'

Bernie turned to Jack and said, 'If you wait here Jack, I will go to the end of the tunnel and call up to you. You can then put a large stick into the ground for Mum to aim for. Please make sure she and Lily can see the stick clearly before you re-join Willie and me in the tunnel.'

'Okay,' replied Jack and went in search of a suitable stick.

'I'll see you later when we join our tunnels together,' shouted Bernie to Madge. 'Good luck with your digging and Lily, be a good girl and keep up with your mum. She will need all the soil removed from behind her and don't forget to spread the soil about.'

'Lily will be fine,' replied Madge. 'You just dig fast, as you have two helpers to my one,' she went on.

'I will,' said Bernie as he headed off to the entrance in the field.

Madge and Lily waited by the small hole Madge had dug. They could not start to dig until Jack had marked the spot she would need to aim for. Willie followed his father into the burrow so he could start to remove the soil as his father started to dig towards his mum. Jack had found a suitable stick and waited for his father to call up to him. Once Bernie had reached the end of his tunnel he called up to Jack. Jack moved a little and called to his dad to shout again. It took a few shouts for Jack to find the right place to put the stick into the ground. Once he had the stick firmly in place, he called to Lily, to check she could see it clearly. She called back saying, she could see it and that he could now head off to help Willie.

Bernie stopped digging after a while and then waited quietly inside the burrow with Willie. They had their ears to the wall facing where Madge would be digging towards them. They would need to rely on their hearing as this was the only way of knowing the exact direction to dig. Madge would need to keep aiming for the stick and once Bernie could hear her digging, he would start to head towards her. Madge would then use her own hearing to aim for Bernie's digging. This method had proved very successful in the past and Bernie could see no reason why this would not be the case again.

A sudden noise behind Bernie and Willie made them both jump and turn around. It was only Jack returning to say that he could no longer see his mum above ground and that he had placed a large stick in the ground where the tunnel ended. He had made sure Lily could see the stick before he left. Now all three waited quietly to see who would be the first to hear Madge digging.

Giganta moles have very good hearing but it seemed an age before Willie said he could hear his mum digging. He pointed to where he felt his dad should dig. Bernie wanted to wait until he could hear Madge and confirm that his son was correct in the direction. *Oh,* he thought, *what it is to be young and still have such acute hearing.* He did not doubt his son's directions but also, he did not want to waste energy digging slightly in the wrong direction. It wasn't long before Jack confirmed the direction but he still could not hear his wife. The twins badgered their dad to start digging and saying that he was getting old and deaf. Bernie reluctantly gave in and started to dig in the direction the boys had indicated.

He dug quickly and the boys were soon pushing this new soil out of the burrow. They resumed their former system of Jack remaining underground while Willie moved the soil away from the entrance and onto the pile. Willie started to put the soil to one side of the mound as it was starting to get very large. He knew the farmer would eventually come across the field to see why he had suddenly got a large amount of soil piled up but he hoped, as they all did, that it would not be until they had finished the emergency exit. They needed to have air flowing through the burrow to ventilate it.

Every now and again Bernie would stop digging to listen. He could now hear his wife through the soil and smiled to himself at how accurate the twins had been in their directions. They were growing up, developing the skills they would need as they got older, but they still had the playfulness of children. *A great age to be,* he thought. *Work when required by the family, a lot of playful fun and no responsibilities.*

Madge was getting nearer. He could hear her clawing at the soil. It was rhythmic. A constant speed. He knew she would be shifting as much soil as he was and he only hoped Lily was scattering the soil around so it would not be obvious where the entrance would be. He knew they would all go to the emergency exit once the two passageways had been completed to ensure the soil was very well dispersed and then the entrance would be covered up. They all needed to know exactly where the entrance was in case of emergencies.

Bernie stopped digging and called out to Madge. She stopped when she heard his voice. They were now very close and he didn't want them to suddenly break through at the same time and claw each other. Madge said she would stop and let him push on.

Bernie pushed on and within a couple of minutes he was sitting next to Madge looking down the tunnel she had dug. Lily was busy moving the last of the soil out of the way while the twins were doing the same from the other tunnel. Once the twins had finished, they all headed down the tunnel to the emergency exit. They checked to make sure all evidence of a hole being dug had been hidden and then they camouflaged the hole. They made a mental note of its exact position, in case they needed to enter their new home from this direction. It would only be in an emergency as they wanted its position completely hidden without any signs of activity.

It was starting to get dark now and they still had not got any bedding sorted out for tonight. They all spread out into the wood to gather bracken, dried leaves and anything else soft they could find. They would then head to the main entrance and take their bedding inside for tonight. The rooms would be dug out starting tomorrow, but for now, they would sleep in the tunnel and pull some twigs across the entrance to stop the draught. They could not hide the hole due to the volume of soil outside and the flatten grass from all the activity today. The farmer will come to see what has been going on and then conclude he has some badgers on the edge of his field. They could only hope the farmer is okay with having badgers. They had not seen any evidence of badgers in the vicinity, when they had looked around the area before deciding to build their home. Admittedly, it was only a cursory look around and they felt sure there would be some badgers in the area.

For now, it was time to relax, have something to eat and then enjoy their new surroundings before going to bed. Tomorrow would be another very busy day, as would the next few, until they get their home fully constructed and furnished.

# 3. Creating Rooms

The sun shone brightly by the time the twins popped their heads out of the tunnel entrance. They were careful to check there was no one around. They peered through the twigs which they had covered the entrance with last night. All was quiet and nobody could be seen in the yard at the farm. They ran into the field licking the grass to get some water that hung in droplets from the individual blades after last night's shower. Madge appeared next asking the twins to be quieter and to go around the back of the pile of earth they had moved yesterday to see if they could find some worms for breakfast.

Bernie followed Lily out last and stood up on his hind legs to stretch, but also to have a good look around. He sniffed the air to see if anything smelt strange. It didn't, plus he could not see anyone at the farm. Bernie led Lily into the wood to see if they could find anything to eat under the wood litter. There should be plenty of insects to find along with the worms and beetles. It was too early to find nuts and fruit but he would be looking out for the plants and trees that would bear these foods later in the year. It wasn't long before they had both filled their pouches with food and headed back to their new home. The twins were still looking and digging in the pile of soil, but they had already given plenty of food to Madge.

Bernie called the twins over and they all went inside to eat the goodies they had found for breakfast. Plans were laid out on the various tasks that lay ahead of them today and who would be doing what jobs. Madge would mark the walls where she wanted the rooms to be dug out. The first to be dug would be the eating area and food store, as this was the most important room. It would be the second room from the entrance on the right. The first would be the toilet, but this could be sorted out later, as they could use the woods for now.

Bernie started to dig out the first room knowing the shape and dimensions Madge wanted. The twins were once again in charge of removing the displaced soil, keeping a constant eye open for food. Madge continued down the tunnel marking the shape of each doorway so Bernie would know where to dig. He would get the dimensions of each room before he started to dig. When Madge had finished marking the walls, she came to see how Bernie was getting on. He had nearly finished digging out the room and it would soon be time for him to move onto another, while Madge and Lily finished the final shaping of the room.

When Bernie had finished the first room he moved into the tunnel. He could just make out the marks on the wall showing where each room was to be dug. He looked at Madge and queried the amount of rooms marked. He was expecting to dig a total of six rooms but he counted eight.

'What's this?' he said.

Madge replied, 'I thought as it was easy digging, we could have a separate room for storing bedding and the children could have a play area for when the weather is really bad.'

'Eight rooms it is,' said Bernie. 'I'd better get cracking and you boys had better get moving the soil otherwise we will not get finished before Summer.'

The boys moaned at the prospect of days of moving soil when all they really wanted to do was go and explore the area.

'No good moaning boys,' said Bernie, 'we need to get a move on and then you can go and explore.'

Once the food store, toilet and main bedroom was complete they took a break to go and collect more bedding material and search for some food. Apart from giving themselves a break from all the digging, they could start to explore the area while collecting supplies. The twins were off like a shot, with Lily running behind them trying to catch up. Bernie had to shout to the twins that they must wait for Lily and look after her. They were also not to roam too far and they must collect food. There was little point in trying to get them to collect bedding material when really all they wanted to do was explore. They would not want to be hindered carry lots of bedding. It will be difficult enough to get them to return with any food.

'We shouldn't moan at them if they don't get any food Bernie,' said Madge. 'They are still young and I would be wanting to explore if I were their age.'

'I suppose so,' said Bernie. 'We had better get a move on and find the bedding and food then before it gets dark.'

Madge and Bernie chatted as they searched but always kept an eye open as to where they were going and also listening for anything that suggested danger. They noticed that although they saw other animals and birds, they disappeared as they started to get close.

'I suppose they all feel threatened by us Madge,' said Bernie.

'What do you expect,' replied Madge. 'They do not know us. They have probably never seen anything like us before and we are larger than most of the animals. It will take some time for them to get used to us and understand that we are no threat to them.'

'We should be getting back Madge,' said Bernie. 'It's starting to get really dark and I don't want the children out in the dark yet. We have not explored the entire area and do not know what is around here that may cause us a problem.'

'You're right,' said Madge and then shouted for the children to came back.

It took a couple of shouts before they replied and were back at the entrance to their home just as the sun dropped behind the woods.

As was expected, the twins and Lily had not brought any bedding back but they did bring some food. It was going to be a nice little feast tonight, as the children had found a hidden stash of acorns. Some poor squirrel will be cursing them, when they find out their stash had been ransacked. Still, they will worry about that another time. For now, they can relax and enjoy some good food. Tomorrow they will continue with the other rooms.

# 4. Meeting the Cows

It was early. In fact, it was astonishingly early for the children to be up and wanting breakfast. They normally have to be dragged from their beds, otherwise they would stay there until lunch time. They kept on at their parents to get breakfast, as they were hungry. It turned out that they really wanted to go and explore the area, but they knew they would not be allowed, until they had had breakfast.

Breakfast was soon wolfed down and they were all clambering to get permission to go out. They were instructed to all stay together and not go too far, as they needed to make sure they would know the way back.

Also, as Bernie explained, 'We do not know the area ourselves or who lives around here.'

With the okay to leave, they were off without a backward glance. They knew they had to be back before dark but that still gave them hours and they could always find some food while they were out.

The twins had just had their fourth birthday and were starting to be allowed a little more freedom for exploring. Willie is the slightly elder twin and is very much like his father. He has dark brown fur and his arms and legs are strong. They would get a little stronger over the next year and he

31

would grow a little more than the 1.2 metres he currently is. He would be a young adult in a year's time and would be able to take on more responsibilities within the household. For now, he is very happy to explore the area and play with his brother Jack.

Willie is a very quick learner of languages and could already talk with most of the animals he has come across. Some of the smaller animals tended to keep away from him and Jack, as they are rather boisterous when they are playing. This gave little chance of learning their languages. Willie's main skill, which he likes to practice every day, is tracking animals. He has this natural ability to sense where an animal is going, but also what type of animal it is. He could also judge roughly how long ago that creature had passed by. He was turning into his father, whether he liked it or not.

Jack is the other twin, who is slightly smaller in height to Willie but has the same dark brown fur. His arms and legs were developing fast like Willie's. He is very laid back and takes life as it comes. He never seems to worry about anything, which is the complete opposite to his father. Jack's special skill is his uncanny ability to find food. He could walk through a wood and suddenly stop, move some wood or soil and un-cover a hoard of nuts that a squirrel had hidden. They don't know how he is able to do this, but they are very grateful for his ability to provide nuts, at a time when they were scarce to find. The other food he is able to track down is fungi. This is their favourite food, a delicacy for giganta moles and a skill they all benefitted from.

Jack is the mischievous one of the family and would lead Willie astray at times, getting them both into trouble. He is also a prankster. He loves to play practical jokes on all the family members. The one he recalls as the best joke, was when he collected a lot of acorns and presented them one night to the whole family as a special treat for dinner. What he didn't tell them was that he had carefully peeled the outer layer off the acorn, removed the juicy inner and then put mud inside, before wrapping the outer skin back in the shape of the original acorn. He fixed the outer skin in place by using resin from a Scots pine tree. He watched as all the others eagerly dived in, peeled the outer layer off and then popped them into their mouths. He fell about laughing as they all spat them out when they tasted the mud. They could not be angry with him for long as they appreciated the skill he had applied to the task, plus, he then provided all the insides for them to eat.

The twins charged off towards the river with Lily shouting at them to slow down, as she could not run as fast as them. The boys waited for her once they had got to the river bank. There were bushes along the top of the bank with gaps that they could squeeze through. Once they reached the other side of the bushes, they stood on top of a steep bank that dropped to a small river which was flowing fairly quickly. They could see weed trailing in the flow of the water but could not see the bottom, as the water was too coloured. They were not sure if this was normal or whether there had been a lot of rain recently in the area.

They decided to head downstream away from the wooded area that housed their back door. There was no particular reason for this, apart from the fact, they could see a large wooded area further downstream and they had already done a little bit of exploring in the wood where they now lived.

They were unable to stay on the river bank all the way as the bushes and trees sometimes went right to the edge and often hung down towards the water. The river flowed fast at times when it shallowed, showing them a gravel bottom and then more slowly, once the water got deeper and murkier. The river twisted and turned as it worked its way across the large field. At the end of the field there was a thick hedge, which reached out over the bank and stopped them from going further. The river was too wide for them to jump, plus they did want to try and cross where it was shallow, as the water moved a little too quickly for them to feel confident, it would not wash them downstream.

They would have to follow the hedge and see if they could find a place where they would be able to crawl under it. That is, if they wanted to keep heading towards the wood. Luckily, they did not need to go far before they found a place. It would be a squeeze and they would probably make the gap larger as they pushed through, but that didn't matter.

With some pushing and shoving from behind, they all managed to get through. This field was very much like the field they now lived in, but this had cows in it. They were black and white with some brown ones as well. There were a lot of cows. A couple near to where they crawled through the hedge looked up from their eating and just stared at them.

'Good morning,' said Willie.

The cows stopped chewing and looked at them in amazement.

'Who are you?' said one of the cows.

'I am Willie, this is my brother Jack and this is my sister, Lily,' said Willie.

'Where have you come from,' said the Cow.

'We have just moved here and are living on the edge of the next field,' pointing to where Willie meant.

'What are you?' said the Cow.

'We are giganta moles,' said Jack.

'We have never seen a creature like you before,' said the Cow.

The other two cows nearby nodded their agreement.

Lily moved a little closer to the twins and then said very quietly, 'Why are all the other cows walking towards us?'

The twins looked up and saw what she meant. The Cow who had been speaking to them turned to see what they were looking at.

She turned back and said, 'Do not be afraid, they will not hurt you. They are curious to see who you are and as they can see we have been talking to you, they feel safe to come over.'

She explained to the other cows who they were and where they were now living.

Lily asked if they would be safe exploring the area, as they did not know who lived here. The cows agreed that apart from the road, which is always dangerous to cross, the only other possible danger was the foxes who prowled the area looking for meat to eat. Jack confirmed a hungry fox would cause them a problem, but not their dad. He was a lot bigger than them and can be very fierce when threatened. He assured the cows that he would not cause them a problem and indeed anyone, as long as he and his family were not threatened. They bid the cows farewell as they wanted to continue their exploration.

# 5. A Deer Encounter

Lily is the youngest of the three children and the only daughter. She is only about 0.7 metres tall and has just had her first birthday. Like her mother she has fairer fur, but this is already starting to darken as she gets older. Whether it would go as dark as her dad's, they did not know. It would be another year before they would know the answer to that. Her body is still growing and her arms and legs are not as strong as the twins, so she is excused some of the heavy chores, that would be required of them in the coming days and weeks. It would not excuse her from helping the others, but she did not as yet, have the strength to dig tunnels and build a home. It would come over the next couple of years.

She is quite a shy child and is not very adventurous, although she does love to follow her brothers and see what they get up to. She always wants to do what they do, but she was on occasion too small and not strong enough to join in. Madge would check to make sure the boys looked after Lily, which they did, generally.

They headed back to the river bank, which now did not have all the bushes along the top. There was the occasional tree but the rest was just long grass. The bank had in places been pushed down by the cows, so they could have a drink from the river. The bottom of the river again could be seen and was gravel. It would make a good crossing, as it was very shallow here. Although the water was moving very fast, Willie felt confident that they would be able to cross without any problems. Willie went first and found the gravel bottom to be very firm. The water flowing past his legs did not cause a problem, so he returned to the bank where Jack and Lily were waiting. Jack entered the water first and then stood by Willie so they could both hold Lily's hands as she climbed into the river. They all walked across the river and up the bank to the other side, without any problems. At the top of the bank they were in another grass field that did not have any animals in it. They walked across this field until they came to the large area of woodland they had seen from where they live. Apart from the cows they had seen, they had not seen any other animals and only a few birds.

The boundary between the fields and the wood was a simple fence of barbed wire, which was easy to get through. They stood at the edge of the wood and looked in. Their ears were listening for any sounds. They heard various birds chirping, but nothing else. It was a disorganised wood with trees growing randomly. Their leaves would soon start to grow and completely cover the branches over the next couple of months. It was very light here but as Spring turns to Summer and the canopy fills in, it would become a lot darker. It smelt of old leaves and rotting wood. It was exciting.

They pushed on into the wood. There would be bluebells here soon as they could see the leaves pushing through the leaf litter.

'This will smell fantastic when they flower,' Lily remarked.

She liked to pick wild flowers and give them to their mother, who always appreciated the gifts and loved to have the smell of flowers indoors. There were brambles in clumps and they noted this for later in the year, when they would provide blackberries. These were always a treat in the late Summer and Autumn. They also noticed that some of the trees were hazel and some sweet chestnut. This really will be a food wood for them later on. Although the children were exploring for their own fun, they also knew the importance of observing where food could be gathered and knowing at what time of the year it will be ready for eating. Their parents will be very glad to learn of this wood.

Just then they heard a noise. It was a little way ahead of them and it stopped their chatter. They froze to the spot. Their eyes were scanning the trees and their ears alert for any clues as to where they should look. The rustle of leaves just to their left and further in the wood gave away the position. It was an adult deer, with a head of antlers still velvety, as they were not fully grown yet, after he had shed them last Autumn. He was unaware that they were there and although his ears kept moving round, he was tucking into a meal of bark that he was stripping from a young tree. Jack called out to the deer, who immediately stopped eating and stood perfectly still. He was working out if he should run away. Jack called again, saying hello and introducing themselves. The deer moved slowly towards them and asked who they were. Jack explained and also what they were, as the deer had clearly never seen a giganta mole before. The deer moved right up to them, once he had determined they would be no threat to him and anyway, he was a lot bigger than them.

He explained that there are about a hundred deer that wandered around the area, staying mainly in the woods, although they did occasionally go into the fields. This generally was at dusk or dawn when there was little chance of any people being about. They told him where they had just set up home and he knew where it was. He agreed that he would call in during the next few days, when it was getting dark to say hello to their parents. He liked to meet newcomers, as he wanted to know who would be moving around the fields and woods. He also believed that those of them that have lived in the area for some time, should greet newcomers and make them feel welcomed. He would also let them know where the possible dangers are and where the other residents live in the area. They said their farewells to the deer and headed off once more, going further into the woods. The deer resumed his eating.

# 6. Rabbits and a Roman Road

The ground started to rise and they crossed little gulley's, that drained the water from the wood when it rained. Bracken was starting to grow here and it looked as though there would be a lot of it. They startled a couple of squirrels as they made their way up the hill, but they soon relaxed as they all chatted briefly, introducing themselves. The squirrels were a good source of information about where they would be able to gather nuts in the Autumn.

They moved on again going over the top of the hill and down the other side. The ground was soft here and they found a rabbit warren. There were lots of holes, but there were not any signs of the rabbits. They called down some of the holes but there was no reply. The holes when they looked closer were partially covered in leaves, which suggested that perhaps this warren was not used any more. They headed off going further down the hill. There hadn't gone far when they the saw a rabbit. He had heard them calling and came to see who they were. Once again, the introductions were done and the explanation of where they had come from and where they lived now. The rabbit explained that they have moved recently from the warren they had just come from because some humans had put netting over the holes and then sent a ferret down the holes. He said that he lost two uncles and three cousins that evening, so they agreed to move and were now building a new home.

The twins were eager to help as they were good burrowers and Lily would help to move the soil away from the entrance. They were led a few hundred metres further down the hill, where there was a large bank rising above a grassy area within the wood. Just beyond the grassy patch, there was a small stream, which was fed by some of the various gulley's they had crossed earlier.

'This little stream does not dry up in the Summer,' said the Rabbit, 'as it is fed from a spring higher up the hill. It makes for a constant supply of drinking water.'

Bobby, the little rabbit, introduced the twins and Lily to his family. It was quite a large family, even though it had just been reduced in size recently. Bobby's mum and dad had already dug one tunnel with an escape route but they needed more, plus they needed to dig out rooms for them to live in.

'This is exactly what our mum and dad are doing back home,' said Lily.

The twins offered to dig a side tunnel, off the main one already completed. Willie would dig the hole while Jack moved the soil to the entrance and Lily moved in away from the entrance. Bobby who was very little, helped Lily. The idea was for Willie to take the side tunnel about 10 metres before coming back up to the surface. He was moving fast through the soil as it was lovely and soft. Jack was having difficulty keeping up with Willie, as he was increasingly having further to go, to move the soil to the entrance. Jack was about to ask Willie to stop for a while, while he cleared what had already been dug when he heard Willie curse.

'What's the matter, Willie?' called out Jack.

'I can't go any further,' replied Willie. 'I have hit something very hard and have tried to go around it but I can't find the end. It doesn't look like soil or smell like it. I am stumped,' he said.

They both headed back down the tunnel and found Bobby's dad. Willie explained what had happened. They all then went down the tunnel to have a look. He sniffed the hard surface and touched it. He turned to Willie and asked if he had tried to go straight up. Willie hadn't tried this, as the tunnel wasn't the required length. Bobby's dad dug up the side of the obstacle and fairly soon came to the top. He was then able to dig onwards again. He kept going and the twins cleared the debris out of the tunnel. When they returned to the top of the obstacle, after numerous trips clearing the soil away, they found that Bobby's dad had disappeared down the other side. He was throwing the soil up to the top of the obstacle, for the twins to clear.

Once they had cleared this, they found Bobby's dad sitting on the top of the obstacle waiting for them.

'What is it?' Willie asked.

'It is a Roman road,' said Bobby's dad. 'They were built many, many years ago and have long been forgotten. They have got buried over the long years since they were built. For us, they are a problem as you have found out. You cannot dig through them. We have a choice of going over or under but you can never go around them, as they have no end. I think that as we have now gone over this one, we will leave it this way and just make an exit from here.'

They quickly dug up to the surface removing the last of the soil. They then slightly covered the entrance with leaves and grass. Time was getting on now and Willie said they had better start heading back. They explained where they lived and Bobby's dad gave them directions for a shorter way back. With farewells and a promise to return to play with Bobby, they headed home via a new route.

The route took them back up the hill and then they veered off to the right going across a densely forested section with very tall straight pines. It was dark in here and they were glad that it hadn't started to get dark yet. It was a scary place and would need further investigation another day. Once they were clear of the darkness, they went across a recently cleared area of woodland before reaching fields. They could see the river two fields away and the small wood that was where they lived on the other side. They headed further to their right, into a lightly wooded area and dropped down to the river via a stone track which the farmer must use. The river could be crossed via a bridge.

It was just a short journey through the wood to come to the edge of the field and their home. Bernie and Madge were sitting outside their home having a drink as their children appeared from behind them. The children recalled their travels and the encounters they had made, along with the information about the areas for gathering food. The story of the Roman road was the best bit, as even their parents had not known about this. While they had been out; both the twins and Lily's bedrooms had been finished. They dashed inside to see their rooms. Now they could start to kit their rooms out how they liked. But not tonight. It was time for dinner and then bed. They had had a tiring day, but a great day. They would fall asleep dreaming about their adventures and future adventures to come.

# 7. An Entrance Filled

The sun shone brightly this morning and the children were still asleep in their beds. They were exhausted after their exploring yesterday and they were so excited last night, that it was not until very late that Bernie and Madge managed to get them all off to sleep. Bernie suggested that they take advantage of the children sleeping in and have a lie in as well. They had made great progress getting their new home constructed and had in fact made all the rooms and tunnels. The large pile of spoil outside their front door was testament to all their efforts. All that remained was for the interiors to be finished along with some furniture. This would be done over the coming days.

Finally, they heard the children start to move around so Madge got up to sort out their breakfast. Bernie lingered a little longer before he too made an appearance. The children were all seated round the table in the eating room. They were all relating stories from the day before and discussing whether they should go back and visit their new friends. Bernie quickly put a stop to this as he reminded them that while he still had some work to do getting all the rooms finished, they must go out and look for food. If they were quick and successful, then they could go and find their friends later in the afternoon.

Once breakfast was finished the children all went and cleaned their teeth before returning to the eating room where Madge gave them their instructions on what food she would like them to collect. They knew also there were other staple foods they could bring back if found, which would be stored. The list was not long and they already knew where to find some items. The others would require a lot more searching, but perhaps they may find someone who could help them. There was still a lot of area around them that they had not yet explored and who knows who lived there.

When the children had left, Bernie and Madge headed off themselves in search of wood from which Bernie would make some furniture. Madge was keen to get some more bedding, as it had not rained recently and she could lay this in the sun to ensure it was completely dry. They worked their way into the wood and away from the river. It was an area they had not visited before, so it was useful from an exploring point of view as well as seeking out what they needed. They would explore properly once their home was complete.

'What's that noise?' asked Bernie.

'I don't know,' replied Madge. 'It sounds as though it is coming from the field where our home is.'

'It does indeed,' agreed Bernie. 'I think we need to go back and check that everything is alright.'

They both headed back to where they had come from a little earlier. They moved quietly and as quickly as they could, but they were very conscious that there may be danger nearby. The noise was getting louder the nearer they got to the field. When they were still a few yards from the hedge, they could see a tractor moving backwards and forwards where they had just built their home. They crept forward very slowly keeping low to the ground to ensure they would not be seen. They crept under the hedge and stopped. They were only about 20 metres from their home and could now clearly see what was going on. The farmer had used his tractor which had a curved metal thing fixed to the front and he was moving all the spoil about so there would be no pile left. In fact, in the process of this, he had covered their entrance with soil. It was impossible to tell exactly where their entrance was. They could only stay where they were and watch the farmer.

Madge started to cry. 'All that hard work we have put in and in just a few moments he has ruined everything for us,' she said.

'Never mind Madge,' Bernie replied, 'the soil will only have gone a little way in. We can go through the back door and dig our way out. We'll have it all done before it gets dark, with the help of the children. The furniture will have to wait another day and so will the bedding.'

It took the farmer another 30 minutes before he was happy with the results of his efforts. He then turned the tractor around and headed back up the field to the yard. He put the tractor in the barn and then went indoors.

'You stay here Madge while I'll go in through the back door,' said Bernie. 'I will call to you when I am on the other side of the soil so you know where I am. You can then start to dig from this side.'

'What if the farmer looks down the field,' said Madge.

'Good point,' said Bernie. 'It would make sense that you hide by the hedge and wait for the children to return. When they have, Lily can look out while you dig from your side and the twins can help move the soil away. It would make sense for the twins to spread the soil so there is no mound. We don't want the farmer back just yet.'

'Be careful,' said Madge. 'I don't want you hurting yourself.'

'I will be careful,' said Bernie.

Bernie headed off into the wood to find the back door. On his way he saw Lily returning with her arms full of food.

'That's a good lot of food Lily,' said Bernie. 'Well done. We have a bit of a situation at home which we will need your help as well as the boys. Where are they?'

'They will be along soon,' said Lily. 'They are still picking some berries but sent me on ahead to let you know we had found plenty of food. What has happened at home?'

Bernie told her of the noise they had heard and when they reached the edge of the field, they had seen the farmer levelling the spoil heap, which has resulted in their entrance being buried.

'I am going to go in the back door and start to dig my way out,' said Bernie. 'Your mother will tell you what she wants the three of you to do. She is by the hedge near our home. I will see you later.'

Bernie easily found their back door and quickly headed into the darkness. He stopped briefly for his eyes to adjust to the total darkness, before heading off. He was so pleased that giganta moles had such good eyesight in the dark. It did not take him long before he was faced with a large pile of soil. He estimated that soil had gone about 1.5 metres into their home. This was more than he thought would be the case and it would mean a lot more digging. He called out to Madge and was rewarded very quickly with the sound of her voice. She told him that the twins were also now with her having appeared only a couple of minutes after Lily's arrival. They were ready to start to dig from their side, now they knew where to dig.

All Bernie could do was pull the soil past him into their corridor so that he could make headway towards the door. Madge started to throw the soil behind her while the twins pushed the soil away, spreading it over the flattened soil the farmer had created. Madge soon found the solid soil, which were the walls of their home. This enabled her to just remove the loose soil the farmer had pushed into the hole. It seemed they had been digging for ages, but eventually after only about 30 minutes, Madge broke through and was greeted with the smiling but rather muddy face of Bernie.

Once the entrance was widened, they were able to start moving the rest of the soil out of the corridor. It took about one hour from start to finish and in all that time, Lily kept watch in case the farmer came out. Bernie inspected how the twins had spread the soil around and was pleased to see that the farmer should not be able to tell from the farm yard, that they had opened up their entrance. It was not the day they had planned, but at least they are all safe and with all the food the children had collected, they were able to have a really good meal. They needed it, as they were all famished. Tomorrow, Bernie and Madge will hopefully do what they had planned today. The twins were already planning revenge on the farmer tomorrow.

# 8. A New Food Source

They awoke to another lovely sunny morning, which was good news for Madge, who hopefully would be able to get more bedding found and dried today. Bernie would get the wood he needed and start to make the furniture. The children, well they would not be telling their parents what they had planned today, because they knew they would not be allowed. Best they are ignorant to their plans for the day.

Surprisingly all the children were up just after dawn and raring to go.

'Why are you all in such a hurry this morning?' asked Madge.

'We want to explore more,' they all said in unison. 'We were unable to yesterday, thanks to the farmer, so we have some catching up to do.'

'Well be careful,' said Madge, 'and be back in good time for dinner tonight.'

'We will,' they shouted, as they run out into the woods.

They followed the hedge towards the farm, but always keeping just inside the wood. The wood came to an end just behind the farmhouse. They could see there was a back garden with a good size lawn and an area fenced off with chicken wire. They could not make out what was inside the fenced

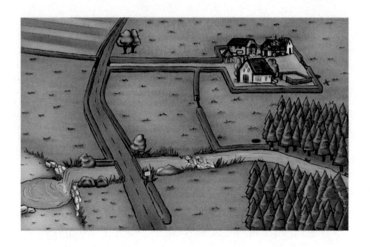

area, which suggested it must want a closer inspection, otherwise, why was it fenced off? They would need to cross a small area of field from the wood to the back garden, which did not have any cover. Lily was again in charge of look out, while the boys were going to investigate the garden. The plan was only to visit the farm and see what mischief they could do as pay back, for what he had done to them yesterday. What this mischief would be, they did not know. They would make it up as they went.

With no movement visible around the house or the farmyard, the twins set off, keeping very low to the ground. They were soon by the fence which separated the field from the garden. It would only take a little digging for them to get under the wire fence. They quickly glanced back to Lily who waved them on. Nothing was stirring around the house. They dug some soil away from the bottom of the fence and found that the wire was laid on the ground to stop them digging straight down. They moved backwards and after about 20 centimetres they were clear of the wire and could then dig underneath.

The soil was firm but not hard enough to cause them any problems. They were soon inside the garden looking at the inner fenced area. They ran across the lawn to the house, where they peered in all the windows, to see if anyone was there. Nothing. Good. They turned to the fenced inner garden while they lent their backs against the brick wall of the farmhouse. The stone was warm from the morning sun and their eyes lit up when they saw what was in the garden. Carrots and parsnips. Their favourites and there were a lot of them. Swedes, cabbage, leeks and oh dear, not their most favourite, brussels sprouts. Still, the rest were good.

One final check on the house and yard. No sign of anyone. They jumped over the fence which was much lower than the one on the perimeter and started to dig up carrots, parsnips and swedes. When their hands were full, they jumped over the fence and pushed the vegetables under the outer fence before going back again. This time they picked a couple of cabbages and some leeks which again they pushed under the fence into the field. They would make one last visit to pick brussels sprouts, not their favourite vegetable. Then they headed back to the field and moved all the food to the woods where Lily was waiting for them. Her eyes lit up when she saw the carrots. They sat chatting and watching the farm while they each chewed on a carrot. It was their reward for some serious scavenging.

They headed back through the woods carrying their "ill gotten" gains home. They hoped their parents would be very pleased with them. Madge saw them coming through the hedge and was surprised to see them so early and also

51

mystified as to what they were carrying. It was not the normal food they gather, but also, they were not asked to get anything today. Perhaps they have found another source of food. All three started to talk at once as to where they had been and to show their mum the food they had brought back. Bernie came out of their home to see what all the noise was about and was greeted with three very excited children, all bearing gifts.

Once they had finished telling their tales Bernie looked at Madge. He shook his head and told them they should not have gone so close to the house and most definitely not to have stolen the farmer's vegetables.

'It was very dangerous to have done that,' Bernie said. 'You could have been caught and who knows what the farmer would have done.'

'But he filled our doorway in yesterday and we wanted to pay him back,' said Jack.

'I understand you are cross with the farmer, but he does not know about us and I would like to keep it that way,' said Bernie. 'He will now want to find out who has stolen his vegetables and he will be keeping a very close eye on all that moves around his house. Let's hope he doesn't decide to come visiting again, because if he sees the opening, he will watch the entrance to see what is living here. In the meantime, we may as well have the food tonight. It will make a change from what we have had recently.'

# 9. A Meeting with Ferrets

That afternoon, when the farmer came home and walked out to his vegetable plot to get something for dinner, he saw all the missing vegetables. He called to his wife and pointed to where they had been dug up. He called his two children, but they both denied that they had anything to do with the vanishing vegetables. He looked closely at the ground and saw claw marks in the soil. He also saw some deeper impressions, which suggested they jumped the fence. He followed where he thought they went and found where they had dug under the fence by the field. He looked across the field but could not see anything to help him. He went back and gathered the vegetables his wife wanted for dinner and then he went indoors. While he was cleaning the carrots and swede, he was trying to work out what would have had the vegetables. He decided he would go into the field after dinner and see if he could follow the trail.

It was just getting dark when the farmer headed into the field. He knew where the hole was under the fence and he quickly refilled it and pegged the wire down as well. He then turned towards the wood and was able to see where the grass had been pushed down. There were also faint claw marks. He followed the trail up to the wood but he could not get through the hedge. Whatever it was, had gone under the hedge. He would come back in the morning and see if he could follow the marks through the wood. He was about to head home, when he remembered the large pile of soil he had flattened yesterday. He wondered if an animal had come back, to open up the large hole, which he had filled in. He walked down the field and was reassured as he could not see another pile of soil. He kept going anyway and stood dumb founded. When he finally got there, he saw the hole was opened up again, but the soil had been spread about, so as not to alert him from a distance. *Surely this was not done by an animal,* he thought. This is very clever and done deliberately. He would definitely come back tomorrow morning, explore the wood for other holes and then get nets and ferrets to explore whatever is under ground. He would chase out the intruders and capture them.

It was early morning. Actually, it was very early. Bernie woke up to a strange noise just outside their front door. He crept out of bed and moved very quietly towards the front door. There was hardly any light coming into the entrance, which suggested how early it was. He could hear human voices outside and they were banging something into the ground very near to their front door. A net then appeared across the doorway and he knew then, that it was the farmer. He intended to put ferrets down the hole, to see what was inside. Bernie had experienced this before. It was just before they moved out of their last home.

Bernie quickly woke all the family up and got together some food that they could have for breakfast, but also enough so they could invite the ferrets to join them. Ferrets were hungry animals and if you can supply them with a good feast, they will then leave you alone. The farmer will think there is no one inside as the ferrets will come out again without any trace of occupants…and they say humans are intelligent!

They settled themselves into the room where they eat and nibbled slowly on the food. They wanted to appear to be at breakfast when the ferrets arrive, so they could invite them to join them. They did not want to be finished.

It was not long before they heard the rustle of leaves as a ferret entered their home and then the snuffling sound as they sniffed the ground for the scent of the occupants. A ferret stuck his nose around the corner and stopped dead. He had not seen any creatures like this before. He was shoved aside as another ferret entered the room. He immediately stopped as well, staring at a strange sight of five creatures sitting eating breakfast.

Bernie stood up and welcomed the intruders. 'Why don't you join us for breakfast,' he said. 'We have plenty and I'm sure we can find something you will enjoy.'

The first ferret said, 'Who are you and what are you doing here?'

'Why don't you join us,' said Bernie, 'and I will explain about us to you.'

They all sat down and started to help themselves to the generous amount of food on offer, while Bernie explained who they were and where they had come from. While they chatted, the farmer was pacing up and down outside wondering where the ferrets had got to. He had scoured the wood behind the large hole but had not found another entrance. He thought it was strange, but could not do anything about it.

'Why are they taking so long?' he said to a mate of his.

'I don't know,' came the reply. 'Perhaps they have found a nest of young rabbits and are eating them.'

'Let's give them another 15 minutes and if they don't re-appear, we will have to dig them out,' said the farmer.

Bernie was aware that the farmer would only wait a short while for the ferrets to reappear before he would start to dig the ground and look for them. Ferrets were renowned for eating young rabbits, when they find them in burrows and can often then fall asleep once they were full.

Bernie pointed this out to the ferrets who agreed that they had better go, otherwise they would lose their home. They left wishing the new residents all the best and hoped the farmer left them alone.

Both ferrets popped out of the hole into the net where the farmer and his mate picked them up and popped them into the cages they had with them.

'Well that was a waste of time,' said the farmer.

'But what has dug this hole?' said his mate.

'I don't know,' replied the farmer, 'perhaps we will never know.'

He kicked some soil into the hole and headed back up the hill to the farmhouse, where they disappeared inside.

Bernie went down the tunnel and out of their back door. He then went back to the field to check that the farmer had really left. When he saw that they had gone, he returned home to let the others know. Once again, he would have to clear the soil out from his home. At least this time it would only take a short while.

They cleared up their breakfast things and Bernie told the children to use the back door today but to be alert the whole time. Once they had gone, Bernie went to start to clear up the mess, when he saw a shadow move across the entrance. He stopped dead and eased back into the first room he came to. *What is the farmer doing,* he thought? He was putting something across the entrance and was banging something into the ground next to it. He was not there long and walked away muttering under his breathe, that this will find out what is using the hole.

# 10. Bernie's Revenge

Once the farmer had left, Bernie crept up to the entrance to see what it was. It looked like a trap of some sort. He would go around and have a look from the other side. Sure enough, the farmer had put a trap across the entrance and covered it with long grass, so it could not easily be seen. He gently removed the stake holding the trap across the hole and then moved the trap away, being careful not to set it off. He laid it to the side of the entrance and went in to tell Marge what he had found.

'What are you going to do with it, Bernie?' she said.

'I am going to take it back to the farmhouse and leave it for the farmer,' he said. 'That should confuse him.'

That night after dark, Bernie walked across the field to the farmhouse and placed the trap outside the backdoor. In the process of this he set off the automatic light that was triggered by his movement. He quickly moved around the side of the house and waited to see if anyone came out. He did not have to wait long before he saw the head of the farmer looking around to see what had triggered his light. His head went back inside and then shot out again. He bent down and picked up the trap. He studied it for a while and then looked around outside. He called inside saying that somebody had removed his trap and placed it by the back door. He questioned the children to see if they were playing a joke on him, but they were adamant that they had not touched the trap or even been down the field to see this large hole.

'It's a mystery,' he said. 'I will have to go and check the hole tomorrow to see what is occurring.'

First thing the next morning, the farmer went down the field with his two children to check on the hole. The soil he had kicked in had been cleared away and there was no sign of the trap and the long grass he had put over the trap, was now in the hedge.

'This is very strange,' said the farmer.

He put the trap back into position and covered the hole again with long grass. They then went back up the field to the farmhouse.

Bernie was hidden on the other side of the hedge and watched the farmer put the trap back. *I need to teach this man a lesson to leave us alone,* he thought. That night he enlisted the help of the twins and once again returned the trap back to the farmer, but not before he had helped the twins steal another lot of vegetables. Once they had what they needed for a couple of good meals, Bernie went up to the back door and placed the trap with a parsnip trapped in its jaws. He then moved across the sensor to trigger the light and hid to see if the farmer would come out again. This time the son opened the door and immediately saw the trap and called his dad to come and see.

'Well I'll be,' said the farmer. 'How weird is this.'

They took the trap indoors and Bernie crept away and joined the twins to help them take their new cache of food back home.

'Tomorrow will be interesting,' said Bernie to his sons. 'The farmer will do something else I'm sure, but what, I do not know. You must all be very careful tomorrow and still use the backdoor. Make sure it is well covered and there are no signs of the soil being flattened. You will need to use different paths to and from the entrance, just in case he decides to look further into the woods.'

# 11. The Installation of Cameras

They were all up early the next morning, expecting to see the farmer first thing doing whatever he had planned for them. There was no sign of him or his children. They waited and waited until mid-morning when the children got restless and gave up waiting. They wanted to explore more and agreed that they would all stay together. They would go through the wood and see what was on the far side. Bernie and Madge would stay at home and continue finishing their home. They had not done anything recently due to all the action with the farmer.

They had had a very good morning getting a couple of the other rooms finished. They stopped for lunch and were having a lazy half hour after lunch when they heard the farmer's voice again. He was talking to his children and was doing something in one of the trees on the edge of the field. The son was helping his dad, handing things up to him in the tree, while the daughter had some strange device in her hands and was pressing some buttons on it.

Bernie and Madge crept out the back door and around to the edge of the field, but a little way up the field so they would not be seen.

'It looks like he is fitting a camera,' said Madge.

'Turn the camera a fraction to the right,' said the daughter in the field, who was looking at a screen on the device she was holding. 'That's it,' she said. 'I can see the entrance and an area of about 20 meters all round. If something does enter the hole, we will be able to see it nice and clearly.'

The farmer climbed down from the tree and came to see what the screen was showing.

'That's brilliant,' he said. 'Now let's get the other two in place before it gets dark.'

They fitted two more cameras up in the trees but these two were further in the wood and pointing in different directions so they covered a large area.

'Now let's see what moves in these woods and around that hole overnight,' said the farmer. 'We will solve our little mystery.'

They packed up their gear, once the daughter was happy everything was working correctly and then they headed home.

'The children will be coming home soon,' said Bernie. 'We need to get to them before the cameras pick them up.'

They headed off in the direction they thought the children would return from, being very careful to be out of sight of the cameras. Luckily for them; their backdoor was not in the sights of the cameras, so they waited there for the children to return.

They heard them long before they saw them and immediately told them to quiet down. If the farmer was about, he would have gone looking for the noise. He would not have recognised the noise as a conversation, but it would be a noise he was not used to and this would make him inquisitive. They told them of the farmer's actions that day since they had gone exploring and showed them where he had placed the cameras.

'What are we going to do about these cameras Dad?' said Lily.

'We are going to move them during the middle of the night when they are asleep,' said Bernie. 'Let's get back and have some food and then have an early night. We will be up again before dawn.'

Bernie woke all the children up very early in the morning, as he was going to need their help, along with Madge. As there were three cameras to move – Madge and Lily worked to remove the closest camera, ensuring the camera was never aimed at them. They had to keep the camera facing the ground so the farmer would not see where they were going until they rigged up the camera in their new locations. The twins set about the next camera and Bernie went around to the field by their front entrance and removed that camera.

Once they had all met up with Bernie, they headed up the field towards the farmer's house. They decided it would make sense for the farmer to have a camera showing the chicken coop in case any foxes came about. Madge and Lily put this camera up. The twins were tasked to put a camera showing the barns in case anyone came snooping around there and the last one Bernie rigged up showing them who was at the door. They carefully ensured that they would not be captured on the screen indoors and then headed home and bed again.

Bernie and the twins went back up to the farmer's house just before dawn and waited for him to come outside. They only had to wait about half an hour for the farmer and his son to come outside. They looked up at the camera facing their front door. The farmer scratched his head and then walked to the barn. He looked around, although Bernie could not say why he did this. Perhaps he was looking for footprints or any clues as to who had moved the cameras. Finally, they moved to the chicken coop. They heard the farmer say that this was an absolute mystery how the cameras got moved, as only they had known the whereabouts of the cameras. He did concede that it made sense to have the cameras where they are, as a security measure for the farm, but who can have done this. He told his son that he had played the tape back from the previous night and it did not show who was moving the cameras. All he saw was the field going past.

# 12. Revenge Escalates

The farmer said to his son that they should go and have a look at the hole at the edge of the field, to see if it had been uncovered again.

'Why?' asked his son.

'Because that is the only strange thing to be happening around here, apart from the moving cameras,' he replied.

When they got there, they could see fresh claw marks in the entrance.

'Could it be possible that whatever lives in here has moved the cameras,' he asked his son.

He replied, 'I don't think an animal could have done this. They would have to be very intelligent and have hands. What creature do you know could do this?'

'You are right,' said the farmer. 'There is no animal I know of that would be able to do this. We will leave the cameras where they are and we can see if there is anything snooping around at night.'

The farmer and his son walked back across the field and as they approached the farmhouse, the farmer turned to look back towards the hole.

He turned back to his son and said, 'I am going to plough the field and fill in the hole again. I will then put up a tent within sight of where the hole is and watch all night. I will catch whatever is down there.'

An hour later, as the giganta moles were finishing their breakfast, they heard a loud noise outside. Bernie crept towards the entrance and saw the farmer in his tractor ploughing the field. He watched as the tractor went up and down the field getting ever closer to their home. Bernie returned saying the farmer looks as though he plans to fill the entrance again as part of his ploughing. Madge queried why he would go that close to the trees and Bernie could only speculate the farmer was a little upset with them.

It did not take long before soil started to come rolling down the tunnel from the entrance. They had quickly put up a little barrier of small branches to stop the soil from entering their toilet area and then going further into their home. The barrier worked, which would save Bernie quite a lot of time when he came to dig the soil out again.

They finished their chores indoors and then they all went outside via their backdoor. Quietly they walked around to the field where their entrance should have been. The whole field had been ploughed and the tractor was disappearing back into the barn near the house.

'This is not going too well, is it?' said Bernie to Madge. 'We appear to have made an enemy of the farmer.'

'I think he is confused and mystified as to what is going on,' replied Madge. 'I'm not sure what the answer is,' she said.

'Well I'm not going to sit around and let him keep ruining our home without some recompense,' said Bernie. 'I suggest we dig up the insides of his barn so some of his machinery collapses into the holes we dig under them.'

'Will that not be dangerous?' said Madge.

'Not if we are careful,' replied Bernie. 'We go after dark tonight once he has checked on the chickens. We will leave the entrance as it is for now, because he will come and check later and again tomorrow morning. We will dig it out when he has something else on his mind, like recovering his machinery.'

They rested that day and then ate early, so they could make their way up to the farmhouse and watch for the farmer to check his chicken before retiring for the night. They also took some food with them, as they had a long night ahead of them. They hadn't got to the top of the field when they heard the farmer's voice on the other side of the hedge. He was talking to his son and heading down towards their home. They all moved closer to the hedge to watch.

When they got to where the entrance should have been, the farmer smiled at his son and said, 'It looks like that has stopped them. I will still come down and watch tonight though, in case they decide to dig it out overnight. I have some night vision glasses, so I will be able to see in the dark.'

'Can I come as well?' said his son. 'I will have a word with your mother,' he replied, 'and if she is okay with it, then yes you can. You will have to be very quiet though, because we do not want them to know we are there.'

They then left and returned to the house.

The giganta moles moved up to the top of the field where they waited for the farmer to check his chickens. The farmer came out and did his rounds as normal, but it was a little earlier than usual.

'He normally checks on everything just before dark and yet tonight he has come out about half an hour earlier,' said Bernie. 'I wonder why?'

They sat still watching the front door.

'Dad, Dad the door is opening,' said Lily.

The others were lying down resting as it was Lily's turn to watch. They had all taken turns, so the others could get some rest.

The farmer came out carrying a bundle of something and a bag on his back. The son then came out and he was also carrying a bundle of something and a bag on his back. They walked into the field and headed across the middle, down towards the stream.

'I will go and see what they are doing,' said Bernie. 'Just wait here until I return.'

Bernie went through the edge of the wood, following the field down towards the stream. He stayed the other side of the hedge, so he would not be seen. He could hear them talking, although they were being very quiet. They stopped on a level with where their entrance should be, but they were some 50 metres into the field. The farmer emptied the bag he was carrying and then erected a tent. It was small but large enough for the two of them to be inside. They went inside once they had finished constructing it and closed the door flaps. They were very quiet. After a little while, they opened one door flap and looked through a pair of binoculars at where the entrance should be. As there was no movement, they closed the door flap again.

Bernie went back to the others and told them that the farmer and his son were on look out at the entrance.

'They will probably stay there all night,' said Bernie. 'This is good for us, although we will need to keep an eye out for their return.'

It was starting to get dark now, so they moved to the other side of the house and round the back of the barn. They kept well away from the cameras, but checked to ensure they were still in the same position they had put them. Once at the back they found an area they could easily get into the building. The front was covered by one of the cameras and as there was no back door, they had no choice but to dig. The soil was soft and easy to dig. Bernie had to dig down about a metre though to get under the foundations, but he was soon going upwards into the barn. The twins moved the soil into a large pile so they could fill the hole in easily afterwards.

Once Bernie was inside, they all crawled through. Lily was tasked with keeping an eye out through the front door, making sure the camera did not see her. They did not want somebody coming into the barn without warning. Then they decided on which machinery they would undermine and hopefully collapse into the holes they dug. There was a big combine harvester which was not going to be used until later in the year. This was a good target as it would not affect the farmer immediately and he would have time to get the machine out before he needed it. Although Bernie wanted revenge, he had learnt over the years that it is best to show people that you are not to be messed with, but they also did not want to cause undue problems for the farmer. They needed to live in harmony with him and his family.

Bernie dug from one side and Madge the other. The twins moved the soil away and started to build a pile behind the front doors. The plan was for the farmer to be greeted with a large pile of soil that he would need to move before he could get into the barn and see what else was waiting for him.

Bernie and Madge worked quickly throwing out large amounts of soil, but also not going too deep. They had to be able to get out of the hole before they got the machine to collapse through the top layer of soil. They went backwards and forwards until a large amount of the ground under the machine had been dug out. Once they were happy with what they had done they all started to rock the machine. It took a little while and then they saw the soil starting to move under the wheels. They all jumped back out of the way as the machine almost gracefully sunk into a hole. It settled with the ground level being about half way up the wheels. The farmer would not be able to drive this out. He will need to dig a slope leading down to the machine and then get a tractor to pull it out.

There was a tractor and a thing for turning hay in the barn, as well as the combine harvester. They picked the tractor next, as this would cause more problems for the farmer, if they ran out of time to see to the third piece of machinery. Bernie knew the farmer had at least one other tractor parked inside the other barn, so he would be able to sort these problems out. It took a good hour for Bernie and Madge to get the tractor to sink as before. They stopped for a rest and they all had something to eat. Lily had said the farmer was still down the field. She had managed to climb up into the loft of the barn, where she could see across the field to the tent, the farmer and his son were in. She could also still watch for anybody approaching the front of the barn.

'One more to go,' said Bernie, 'so let's get cracking and then we can go and get some sleep.'

This last piece of machinery only took about 20 minutes to sink into the ground. Lily was called back from the loft and went out after Madge and was then sent to look round the front again. Bernie pulled some planks over the hole they had made and was able to get some bales of hay on top as well. This was so they could push the soil back in and up to the planks without moving them. This hopefully will then not leave too much soil outside the barn for them to disperse. They would then brush over the ground and scatter anything loose over the recently dug soil to conceal what they had done. The twins had worked tirelessly all night moving the spoil and in fact had managed to build a mud wall inside the front doors to a height of two metres. A tremendous job done, which both Bernie and Madge admired before they disappeared down the hole and out of the barn.

With everything back as best they could, they all headed back to their home the same way they had come. They all took one small detour and that was to the hedge near their front door to look out into the field and see what the farmer and his son was up to. The door flap opened briefly and they saw the binoculars. The door flap shut again and all was quiet. They headed home and collapsed into bed. There would be no early rising this morning as it was nearly dawn now.

# 13. A Surprise for the Farmer

The sun was very high when the giganta moles surfaced. It could not be said, it was breakfast time, as it was more likely to be brunch time. They were however, all very hungry. They had had a very tiring night, but they had a very successful night and now they needed to see what the farmer would do.

After brunch they eagerly headed out to see if the tent was still there. It was but the door flaps were open and they could see that there was nobody inside. They headed up the field and then pushed through the hedge near the top where they could look at the farmhouse. All was quiet and apart from seeing the farmer's wife looking out of the kitchen window, they did not see anyone.

It was late afternoon before the farmer came out of the house and walked across to the barn. He opened the doors and just stopped, staring at the huge mound of soil in front of him.

He let out a very loud scream of, 'NOOOOO. What is happening here? Why are all these things happening?'

The farmer's wife, son and daughter all came running out of the house and over to the barn to see what the matter was.

'Who could have done this?' said the farmer's wife.

'I don't know,' replied the farmer.

'Perhaps it was the same people who moved the cameras,' said the son. 'Perhaps it was what is living in the large hole you keeping filling in, in the field.'

'That's impossible,' said the farmer. 'Whatever lives in that hole, surely could not do this?'

'Where has all the soil come from?' asked the daughter.

'I don't know,' replied the farmer.

They walked round the barn and could not see any obvious places where they had entered. The barn was not locked but again there was no sign of anyone moving soil and packing it inside the doors.

'Why don't we check the tape from last night?' said the son.

'That's a good idea,' said the mother. 'I will go in and check the tape while you start to move the soil,' she said to her husband.

They both went off in different directions while the son and daughter waited by the barn doors. The farmer soon arrived with the tractor parked in the other barn. He had put the bucket on so that he could use it to scoop the soil up. He would move the soil to the side of the barn for now. It was such a large pile of soil he was still shifting it when his wife reappeared. He stopped the tractor so she could talk to him.

'There is nothing on the tape,' she said. 'There was absolutely no movement outside the doors last night. In fact, there was nothing showing on all the cameras.'

The farmer's son then called out to his dad. 'Dad, come and see inside the barn.'

He had climbed up the pile that was left and was now standing at the top looking into the barn.

'What can you see son?' asked the farmer.

'I see a combine harvester, a tractor and the hay turning equipment all sunk into the ground.'

The farmer then scrambled up the pile to join his son and stood open-mouthed at the sight below him.

'That's not possible,' he said.

'What isn't,' cried his wife.

'Come and see for yourself,' he said.

He climbed down a little and held his hand out to his wife to pull her up. The daughter, not wanting to be left out, scrambled up as well.

They all stood at the top, dumbfounded. There was no sign of entrance or exit from the barn and yet someone or something had dug out the soil from under three pieces of equipment and piled it up in front of the doors. *This is going to take me some time to sort the barn out,* thought the farmer. *How can I find out what has caused this and why would they do it anyway?*

He finished moving the soil before calling it a night. On his final check before retiring he left some carrots and parsnips out near the chicken run. It was in view of the camera and he wanted to see if and what would take it. One final glance around the area and he went inside. He made a drink and sat down in front of the screen watching the chicken run.

Bernie and the twins had spent the afternoon watching the farmer and his family discover their work from the previous night. They all laughed at various stages, as they discovered what they had done. The farmer was clearly perplexed and was concerned at what was happening to his farm. They had not found where they had dug into the barn, which was good, as it left a further mystery for them.

They watched the farmer check on his chickens and then were amazed at what he did next. He placed some parsnips and carrots on the ground near the chicken run.

'Who has done that?' Bernie commented.

'Perhaps it is a peace offering to us Dad,' said Willie.

'Surely not,' replied his dad.

'Well I think we should take advantage of his hospitality,' said Jack. 'I like a nice carrot and Mum really likes parsnips.'

'Very well,' said Bernie, 'but we must be careful as they are in view of that camera.'

They all moved round to the side of the house and en route they had picked up a long branch that was laying on the ground. There was a fork near the top, which hopefully they will be able to hook over the vegetables and pull them towards themselves, without being in view of the camera. With a little persuasion they were able to gather all the offerings without showing themselves.

Inside, the farmer called to his wife, saying something was moving the vegetables. She looked at the screen in wonderment. How clever. They are using a stick so they will not be seen.

'Would you be able to see from the bathroom window?' she said.

'I'm not sure,' said the farmer, 'let's go and see.'

They quickly went upstairs and without turning on any lights they slowly opened the window. He stood on a chair and leant out looking directly down below him. There were three brown creatures covered in fur. The largest, and it was large, was much bigger than a Badger and nothing like he had ever seen before. This creature was using the stick to drag the vegetables towards them. The two smaller animals then gathered them up. Once they had them all, they moved quietly off and headed into the woods where he lost them in the darkness and undergrowth.

'Well,' said the wife. 'What did you see?'

The farmer explained what he had witnessed, although he was still finding it hard to believe his own eyes. Perhaps these were the creatures that had dug the hole in the field, stolen some of his vegetables and then did the damage in the barn. All these things happened after he had filled in the hole in the field the first time. Each event got worse after he had done something to them. He decided he would leave them alone and not sow the field right up to their hole. If nothing else happens to his farm, then he would conclude, it was these creatures and they were only retaliating for what he had done to them. Time would tell.